CHARLIE
and the Christmas Kitty

For everyone who's ever loved a dog.
—R.D.

Charlie and the Christmas Kitty

Text copyright © 2012 by Ree Drummond
Illustrations copyright © 2012 by Diane deGroat
All rights reserved. Printed in the United States of America.
No part of this book may be used or reproduced in any manner whatsoever without written permission except
in the case of brief quotations embodied in critical articles and reviews. For information address HarperCollins
Children's Books, a division of HarperCollins Publishers, 10 East 53rd Street, New York, NY 10022.
www.harpercollinschildrens.com

Library of Congress Cataloging-in-Publication Data
Drummond, Ree.
Charlie and the Christmas kitty / by Ree Drummond ; illustrations by Diane deGroat. — 1st ed.
p. cm.
Summary: Charlie, a basset hound who considers himself to be
"King of the Ranch," finds an unexpected Christmas gift under the tree.
ISBN 978-0-06-199657-3
[1. Basset hound—Fiction. 2. Cats—Fiction.] I. deGroat, Diane, ill. II. Title.
PZ7.D8277Cg 2012   [E]—dc23   CIP   AC   2011026151

The artist used Winsor & Newton watercolor paint over digital art on
140 lb. Arches hot press paper to create the illustrations for this book.
Typography by Rachel Zegar
12 13 14 15 16 LP 10 9 8 7 6 5 4 3 2 1 ❖ First Edition

CHARLIE
and the Christmas Kitty

by Ree Drummond
illustrations by Diane deGroat

HARPER
An Imprint of HarperCollinsPublishers

Well, howdy!

Charlie the ranch dog here, reporting from the country.

Things have sure been busy around here these days. This evening, for instance, I'm bringing this great big TREE into the house.

Well . . . I'm helping, anyway.

Wow. This BIG TREE is BIG WORK.

It sure is a good thing I'm here! I'm Charlie the ranch dog, after all.

I'm such a hard worker, some people even call me King of the Ranch.

I like the title. It suits me.

After all, I'm the best cattle wrangler, critter chaser, fence fixer, and fish catcher in six states.

Maybe even seven.

Yep, looks like I've got this situation well under control. I think I'll go ahead and get a little shut-eye. Tomorrow's going to be a big day around here.

Huh? What'd I miss?
And WHAT is that NOISE?

DING!

Why, it's a . . .
It's a . . .

It's a **RABBIT!**

Um . . . HELLO?

I believe rabbits are supposed to RUN when dogs chase them?

Hold on just . . . one . . . minute.
Rabbits don't MEOW.

Wait. I don't think that's a rabbit at all.

Meow...

I think that's a
KITTY!

I have to say, I really wasn't expecting this development.

This is by far the weirdest thing that's happened since the girls dressed me in that pinafore.

I'd better go back to sleep and pretend this never happened.

ZZZZZZZZ . . . ZZZZZZZZZ . . . ZZZZZZZZZ . . .

Huh? What'd I miss?

Oh. Whew! It was all just a bad dream.

There's no kitty after all!

My soul rejoices.

Uh oh. This isn't good.
This isn't good at all.

Well, the last thing I'm going to do is
let this whole kitty thing disrupt my peace.
I have a lot of work to do around here!

Maybe if I just mind my own business
and eat my lunch, it'll go away.

Maybe not.

Maybe if I take a nice, long nap, it'll go away.

Maybe not.

Okay, fine. This clearly isn't working.
I'll have to try another approach.

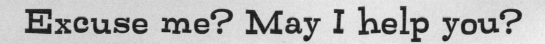

Excuse me? May I help you?

Ahh. That's kinda nice.

You know, this kitty's actually pretty handy to have around! All this ranch work is pretty hard on the ol' back, after all. I guess the kitty can stay.

I hereby proclaim it.

I sure am glad I got this whole kitty business
straightened out.
Now things can finally get back to normal around here!

Charlie's Favorite Christmas Cookies

Makes 24-36 cookies
(Depending on the size of the cookie cutter)

Be safe! Always cook with an adult. Don't touch sharp knives or hot stoves and ovens! And always wash your hands before and after cooking.

Ingredients

Cookies

⅔ cup shortening

¾ cup sugar

½ teaspoon grated orange
    or lemon zest

½ teaspoon vanilla

1 egg

4 teaspoons whole milk

2 cups flour

1½ teaspoons baking powder

¼ teaspoon salt

Egg-Yolk Glaze

1 egg yolk

1 teaspoon water

2-3 drops food coloring

White Decorative Icing

1 (2-pound) bag powdered sugar

¼ cup whole milk

2 tablespoons meringue
    powder (optional)

Instructions

1. Cream shortening, sugar, orange or lemon zest, and vanilla thoroughly. Add egg and beat until light and fluffy. Add milk and mix.

2. Sift dry ingredients together, then blend into cream mixture. Divide dough in half (or thirds, if you double the recipe) and slightly flatten between two sheets of waxed paper. Refrigerate for 1 hour (or freeze for 20 minutes).

3. While dough is chilling, combine egg yolk, water, and food coloring to make the egg-yolk glaze.

4. Roll out dough on a lightly floured surface and cut into shapes with cookie cutters. Transfer shapes to a lightly greased cookie sheet and paint cookies (using a soft brush) with egg-yolk glaze.

5. After brushing with egg-yolk glaze, bake at 375 degrees for approximately 6 minutes. Do not allow the cookies to brown.

6. While the cookies are baking, mix powdered sugar, milk, and meringue powder (optional) to make the decorative icing. Remove cookies from the oven to a wire rack to cool.

7. Using a pastry bag or freezer bag, pipe with white icing to decorate.

Note: When making the white decorative icing, make sure that it is thick and somewhat retains its shape.